Femboy Sorority

- An LGBTQ+, Femboy, First Time, Feminization, Short-Read Romance

by Barbara Deloto and Thomas Newgen

To purchase another copy of this book, or to see our other books go to
https://www.amazon.com/Barbara-Deloto/e/B00J21HWA4/

A few of our other books
Realizing Jessica - A Femboy Gets Fem and Discovers Inner Passions and Love
Desires- Fantasy Becomes Reality for an Occasional Crossdresser
Trannies - Two Guys Get Fem
Jessica's Turn: A Gender-Bending LGBT Romance
Frat House - A Gender-Bending LGBT Romance
*Finishing School - A Boy Is Sent to a Girls' Finishing School - An LGBT
Romance*
All Dolled Up: A Student Gets Fem - An LGBT Romance
Sissy Boyfriend
Being Candy
Paying My Dues
Virtual Vacation
Filling in For Her
His New Dress
Her Gift to Him
Telling Her
Feminized to Win
Crossdreaming
Feminized by Her
Taking it for the Team
Feminized Men: A Guide for Increased Joy in Crossdressing
Feminized Vacation
The House of Enchanted Feminization
Heirs to Heiresses
Connected
Our Gift to Each Other
Girlfriend
Insatiable
A New Taste for Life
Spellbound
Femboy Guild

1

"Hey, look at this!" I grabbed Franny's hand and tugged. I pointed at the picture. "The old sorority house is rebranding. They had too many problems with catty girls not getting along. This summer they're calling for all-male occupancy."

Franny laughed. "Look at it. That old Victorian looks like a cupcake—plum scrollwork around the roof lines, mauve-painted siding, pink porch… What guys will want to live there, Pat?"

"Read on, silly." Fran leaned in and read the description and requirements. "Hmm, must be interviewed. No macho men allowed, must have a more feminine leaning. Okay, that makes sense, considering the way the house is, I guess."

"Right! That's us. Not macho, feminine-leaning." I flicked my hair back and tapped my long, painted fingernail on the bulletin board posting, then pulled a tab off the side with the phone number. "Read the bottom yet?"

Fran scoffed, took out lip gloss and applied it as he read it. "Hmm, okay, so they want to fill the house for the summer and will pay anyone living there to work on it too. I like that idea. I didn't want to go home and work at my shitty summer job anyway."

"Exactly. Me either, plus we can spend the summer together. How great is that? Then next year we don't have to worry about where we're staying. We'll be with other guys like us too. Finally, a place where we can be comfortable to be who we are."

"I guess."

"Let's go there and see it. Maybe we can interview too."
"Why not?"

Off we went from the main campus. We walked through the side streets, the air fresh and laced with scents of hyacinths and lilacs and freshly cut grass. Fran gazed from one big old Victorian frat house or sorority to another. "Gorgeous day, isn't it?"

"Perfect. Look, there it is."

"It's huge. And actually, a pretty nice old house. Very girlish, though, for sure. Bet it's just as girly inside."

We walked up the long slate walk from the street. The house showed a need for some fresh paint, and the flowerbeds needed to be cleaned up. "I see what work we'll be doing."

"Not bad, though. It'll be fun to bring the old girl back up to snuff."

We climbed the porch steps to the tall double front doors that were wide open, letting in the fresh air. I knocked on the door and stood there. "Anybody home?" The foyer was gorgeous, with a sweeping curved staircase leading upstairs. "Hello?"

I heard the click of heels on the parquet floor as a pretty young lady in a pinstriped mini skirt suit and high heels approached, beaming a big smile. "Hello, boys. I'm Jackie." She flung her hand out. We shook it and introduced ourselves.

"We saw the posting. Are we too macho to be a part of this house?"

She looked us up and down and grinned. "Not at all. Not at all, ladies."

"Ladies?" Fran demanded.

"Well, would you rather I call you men? Is that the macho coming out in you?"

I jabbed Fran in the ribs. "No, right. Ladies is fine. What will the rent be?"

"Minimal. A benefactor has taken over the house. He's the one who kicked the sorority out and dictated the new rules. He's where the money for the cleanup wages and materials and clothing budget will be coming from. I've been working with the local retailers to get deals on the outfits for all the ladies who will be living here."

"I thought this was gonna be a place for more feminine guys," Fran said.

"Yes. Feminine enough to be called ladies and... feel very...*pretty* all the time." She winked. "As you'll both be, unless of course you don't want to stay here for next to nothing and live with like-minded girls. If you're too macho for that, just say no."

We looked at each other. Fran's face was red. "What do you think, Pat? I'm not sure we'd be able to go as far as being girls full time. I mean, it's fun to dress a little more feminine, but all the time?"

I looked at Jackie, who stood there, smiling and taking us in. She was hot, and she had a great smile. I grasped Fran's hand and looked into his pretty, eyelinered eyes. "So? I mean, I guess it's just taking what we wear a little further. Paying practically no rent is awesome, too, and it's not like you don't look good in heels and a skirt."

"Pat, stop telling Jackie how I look in heels."

Jackie patted Fran's shoulder. "Franny, it's good that you look great in them. See? You'll have no trouble obeying the rules requiring presentation as girls. Your names feminize well, and your voices are nearly perfect. Using your polite voices will be fine."

Fran shrugged. "I don't know. So how much is the rent?"

"One hundred dollars a month, which we use to buy alcohol and snacks for the bar. We will provide the first full wardrobe, but we don't pay for clothing beyond that. You can add to the wardrobe as you wish. Please, come into my office; you can sign the papers, and we'll get you started. You'll do well, I'm certain of it. Don't be nervous. You'll end up loving it."

She took my hand in her soft manicured hand and led us, with me tugging Fran behind me. Her hips were just slightly flared, and she was a little taller than me in her heels. Her bottom swished in her tight skirt with each minced step. She went behind her desk and sat down.

She took out two packets of paper from a drawer and slid them to us as we sat in front of her desk. "Okay, ladies. Sign and date the acceptance of the bylaws and terms, and you can move in today if you want. Turn to the last page."

We turned it.

"See? There's the rent. Just sign and date and you're all done."

Fran started to read from the beginning. I signed mine and dated it. "Fran, just sign it. It's just a bunch of frat house rules and stuff. Right, Jackie?"

"Right. Just the basic rules so everyone's on the same page. I'd call it more of a sorority than a frat, though. It was a sorority before too."

I nodded. "Of course." I took the packet from Fran, folded it to the last page, and put it down before him. I put the pen on it. "Just sign it and let's have a look around."

"Yes, sign, and I'll give you two a tour and show you your room. Since you're the first ones, you get the other large bedroom with the ensuite bath next to mine. It's lovely."

Fran signed and I tossed both packets to Jackie. She filed them in a wooden file cabinet and locked it. "Smart move. Right this way, ladies."

She led us around the house. The interior was impeccable and needed very little work. The furnishings were a mix of Victorian and modern, but all gave the rooms a very feminine appeal. It was going to be like living in a princess' castle. When we were done, we saw the grounds, tennis courts, pool with the gardens, and the patio out back. It was like a resort.

Back inside, Jackie poured us iced tea after we entered through the kitchen. "Okay, two more things. I'll need your measurements and shoe sizes, of course, so we can get your clothes set up in your room, and then I'll give you the place to go for a blood test. No big deal, no fasting needed. Just a quick blood test to be sure you're safe."

I looked at her quizzically. "Blood test?"

She took a pad from a drawer and a cloth tape measure and began to measure Fran and write the numbers down. "Of course. You wouldn't want to be living with eighteen or so other girls if they weren't tested, would you?"

I asked again. "Tested for what?"

"STDs, of course. You don't want to catch something from a shared toilet seat or somewhere, do you?"

"Uh, right. Of course." I rolled my eyes to Fran and shrugged. "It's too good a deal to not do what we need to. I'd do anything to live here at that price."

"Good attitude, girl. Just what I wanted to hear you say. That attitude will serve you and all your sisters here very well. Let me get pictures of you both for your files."

2

We walked out of the mansion and down the slate walkway back to the sidewalk. Fran looked back to be sure we were out of earshot. "Did you even *glance* at that agreement we signed? Blood tests for STDs?"

"So what? Who cares? Look at the place. It's palatial. Cheap-as-hell rent, and all we have to do is wear clothes that are a bit more feminine, and they even provide them."

"Yeah, they're gonna dress us up as girls and then have us have sex. Why else the STD test? I saw where any violation of the rules is also cause for eviction and that we consent to publication of before and after photos."

"Is that why she took our pics?"

"Yup. I'm sure she'll have pics of us fully feminized too. We'll be stuck obeying any stupid rules they have."

"It'll be worth it."

"Worth it for you to be used by real men? Worth it for you to have to suck guys off? Worth it to be turned into fully feminized, sissy bimbos?"

"Oh Fran, don't be silly...*girl*." I laughed. "Besides, it's not like we haven't done anything like that before. Remember my last birthday party and all the petting going on? I know you had fun. I did. We help each other out that way all the time when we cuddle."

"Petting doesn't require an STD test. Petting isn't my bottom being pummeled."

"Just relax. I'm sure it'll be fine. No one's going to make you do anything you don't want to. As soon as we're fully feminized and living the dream in the princess' mansion, you'll love all of it. It'll be heavenly, *girl*! It'll be so much better than just being a couple of femboys. Right?"

"If you say so. I sure hope so."

"Don't be such a worrywart and stop looking a gift horse in the mouth. Whatever that means."

We walked back to the dorm, drove to the lab and had the blood drawn, then went back and packed our things up. There was no point in not moving in right away, so we just made a couple of trips with the car, and it was done.

We loved our room all done up in frills and floral fabrics, with fresh flowers on the table and the sweet breeze blowing in. We went down to the kitchen, and Jackie was there. "That was quick. Now relax and settle in. Your clothes will be here soon. I already ordered them, and they'll be delivering them shortly. Have a drink from the bar. Relax a little out back. Enjoy your new space!"

"Thanks, Jackie."

"Want to go to dinner with me tonight? The chef hasn't started yet, and the kitchen isn't stocked."

"Chef? There'll be a chef?"

"Our benefactor insisted on it. Nothing but the best for his girls, he said."

"Nice. See, Fran? Heaven."

Fran shrugged. "I need that drink."

Jackie gave Fran a little push on his shoulder. "Go, sweetie. Go get some drinks with your girlfriend and relax in the garden. When your clothes are here, I'll let you know. If you want to shower or take a bath and shave your bodies before you change, that would be good; then you'll be ready to dress so we can go to dinner. It's only one thirty, so there's plenty of time yet. I expect the clothes in a couple of hours."

I took Fran by the hand and led the way to the bar. It was fully stocked already, and we made a couple of Long Island iced teas. Fran was still nervous. I held his hand and looked into his eyes. "Okay, now. Just get used to it. As a matter of fact, we should be using different pronouns for each other, and you can call me Patty instead of Pat." I rubbed the back of her hand.

"Patty. I like that for you. Franny and Patty. Okay... *girl.*" Franny laughed.

"That's the spirit. Enjoy this. Don't be such a stick-in-the-mud. You know how much you like to be feminine. I can't wait to see the clothes Jackie got us."

"I *am* very much looking forward to that. All pretty and sexy and sensual. Mmm. Lovely. Not so sure about leaving the house that way, though." Fran kissed my cheek.

"We'll do fine leaving the house. Now just relax and imagine yourself looking like your dream girl and feeling all feminine and pretty. Let's go outside and drink these. It'll help you chill."

I took her hand and led her out, her flip-flops clopping as we walked. I grabbed her tight bottom and squeezed it in her short shorts. "Nice ass, girl."

"Oh gosh. Not already." She brushed my hand off her bottom.

"Why not? I like touching you. You get so flustered and shy." I squeezed her bottom again, then slapped it.

"Ow! Stop." She sat down on the wicker sofa on the patio in the shade. I flopped next to her and slid my hand on her thigh. "You could use a shave. I feel a couple of stubbles."

"I will." She pushed my hand away. She looked me up and down and sipped her cocktail. "Mmm, you made these good."

"I know. All the better to get you in the mood."

"Oh, stop already! Look at you all hard in your shorts. How ungirly you look."

I took her hand with its long, painted nails, placed it on my hardness, and pressed up against it. "Yeah, that's for you, miss. Uh-huh." I gave her a peck on the cheek and let her hand go. She rubbed me for a while, then crossed her leg and bounced a foot, sipping her drink. "It is lovely here. Gorgeous, actually. I love it."

"Good. I want you to be happy here with me."

We enjoyed the fresh air and snuggled together on the couch as we drank. I started to feel relaxed and a little buzzed, and I knew Fran would be too. "Feel nice?"

"Yes, mmm."

"Me too. I think I want to take a bath in that big old tub and shave my body nice and smooth before our clothes get here."

"I'll shave in the shower. You can have the tub. I know you like that better."

"Deal." I looked at my watch. "Oh heck. I can't wait. I wanna get this going. I'm gonna go in. You?"

"Okay."

I stood and offered my hand to Fran to help her off the couch, and she took it. We walked in hand in hand and went to our suite. I ran the bath, and after it was full, Fran showered. They had perfumed soaps, shampoo, bubble bath, and beautifully scented body lotion. By the time we'd finished, we were both silky and sweet-smelling, our hair was redone, curled with hot irons and styled femininely. We did our makeup completely, with contouring, eyeshadow, and full painted pouty lips. We painted our finger and toenails. By the time we were done, standing in our short satin robes, Jackie knocked. "Clothes are here, ladies!"

I opened the door, and Jackie's eyes went wide. "Oh wonderful, you girls are ready... and you did your makeup. How nice!" She moved aside, and four people carried in the clothes; she directed them where to put everything. "It's all been laundered and is ready to wear. The place we're going for dinner is a bit fancy, so keep that in mind and wear a nice dinner dress, stockings, and heels. Bras, panties, and gel breast-forms are in the dresser. Make a nice cleavage with the gel forms. They have a slightly tacky back so you can do that easily."

The others left. Jackie took a look around. "Like I said, the hosiery and panties and such are in the dresser. You and Fran are pretty much the same size, so the dresses, miniskirts and clothes are anyone's. You'll know whose shoes are whose, and even those are only a half size different. You girls are almost like twins. That's so cute."

She stood smiling. "Everything good? Need anything?"

We shook our heads, still in shock at all the clothes.

"Good. I'll go dress for dinner and meet you downstairs at the bar when you're ready. We can have a cocktail before we leave, if you like, and then maybe you won't be so nervous going out this way. I assume this will be the first time that you two have fully presented as women in public?"

We both nodded, jaws open, eyes wide.

"Yes, I think you should have a drink before leaving. You look like two deer in the headlights. See you downstairs, ladies. Oh, don't forget the perfume. It's in the dresser too."

Franny and I went into the closet and started going through the dresses and other clothes. It was incredible. I wanted to try it all on. Everything was so stylish, sexy, and feminine. The minidresses and skirts were all non-clingy and had at least a somewhat flared hem so any protrusion of maleness wouldn't be seen. I could be hard in my panties in any of them, and no one would ever know. Nice.

I found a seductive, chiffon-overlay, black minidress with a V-neck. I selected it and a pair of five-inch-heel, strappy, black patent stilettos to go with it. I found sheer black stockings, garter belt, a matching bra and panties, and the gel breast forms and placed them on the bed.

Fran was already slipping on a pair of sheer suntan pantyhose; she had cut some of the gusset out of them to allow her male parts to be free, and she slid a sheer black pair of panties over them, trapping her obvious hard-on. She put on her bra and filled it with the forms, then slid on a pair of strappy silver stilettos with five-inch heels. She walked to the mirror and put in her earrings as I slid on my silky stockings and attached them to the garter belt. I slid the panties up over my throbbing shaft and put on the bra and forms. It was all so incredibly sensual and feminine feeling. I was in heaven.

Fran went into the closet and came back with a silver-topped, black-skirted minidress with a V-neck. "Is this good?"

"Fabulous."

She held it against her and smoothed it down. "Not too short?"

"Nope. Just plain sexy, hun. You'll look fabulous."

"Thanks."

I slid on my dress and zipped the back up. I adjusted my cleavage and went to the mirror to put in my earrings, and then I picked out some coordinating bracelets, necklace, and rings. I sprayed perfume under my dress and over my body. I felt like a dream as I looked into the full-length mirror and took in my presentation. I was stunning.

Fran came over and stood next to me. She put her hand on my shoulder. "We do look hot. Better than normal. Much classier and more formal. I think this girl thing is gonna work out just fine. No one will know we have something special under our dresses."

"I think so too. We do look better this way. We should have done this all the time. It feels so right. Go figure."

"I guess we needed to be forced a little, huh?" Her hand drifted to mine as we looked in the mirror. She turned toward me. She ran a finger over my forehead and moved a stray hair. "You're gorgeous, Patty. You're the girl of my dreams."

My eyes roamed her face, taking her new beauty in. "So are you." I slid my hand to the front of her dress and squeezed her hardness as I kissed her neck. She grabbed my bottom tight, pulled me to her, and lifted a leg to rub it between mine. She breathed in my ear. "You are so sexy, girl. I love you." I rubbed her hardness and sniffed her perfumed hair. "Mmm, lovely."

We started to get into it, and our breathing got quick as we caressed each other. I pushed her back, my hand on her breast. "Oh god, we better stop."

"Yes, let's go get a drink. We have to go out in public as two horny girls like this."

We packed our purses and went downstairs.

3

Jackie sat at the bar, her sheer stockinged legs crossed and a strappy stiletto bouncing. A full smile filled her lovely made-up face, and she slid off the stool to go behind the bar. "You girls look incredible. Dirty martini?" She grasped a chilled pitcher and a martini glass.

Franny sat and crossed her legs. "Please."

I sat, crossed my legs, and placed my purse on the bar. "Sounds great, Jackie. Thank you. And thank you for the great clothes. They all look so nice, and I can't wait to try them all on. I didn't see any jeans, shorts, or pants, though. Can we still wear them?"

She placed our drinks in front of us and came around and stood between us. We turned to face her. "No jeans, pants, or shorts. Sorry. You do have some skorts and rompers for when you're climbing ladders and doing things requiring that kind of modesty. Are you two working here this summer?"

We both nodded. I said, "It's great you offer that option. I hated my summer job at home. I assume painting the outside and doing garden work are some of the tasks?" I clinked my drink to hers that she held out to us.

"They are. You can both start tomorrow if you like. Or you can relax for a while first."

Franny shook her head. "We want to start right away. We can only sit around and do nothing for a little while, and then we get bored."

"Wonderful. You can start by painting the siding. We're going from that awful seventies mauve color to cream instead. It might need two coats. We'll see. We want the house to still have a feminine feel but not look like a cupcake. We want it to be classier."

We chatted and leisurely sipped our drinks, then we took turns going to the ladies' room, and when we were all done, Jackie led us to her car. It was a BMW 750iL. A huge, luxurious sedan. I sat in front with Jackie, and Franny sat in back. Franny leaned forward and asked, "So, Jackie, are you a student? What's your role in the sorority?"

"I was a student. Then when I graduated, I started working for our benefactor, and he gave me the task of starting our new sorority in that wonderful mansion. It was a dream come true. I was a girl just like you girls are now, and the opportunity to make more of us excited me to no end."

Franny and I looked wide-eyed at each other. Franny covered her mouth. I turned to look at Jackie while she drove. She was like us? I'd never have guessed. It excited me to think of it. I bounced a crossed leg and absentmindedly caressed my stockinged thigh. "So that's the idea? To turn femboys into girls? Why?"

She glanced at me, then placed her soft hand on my thigh and caressed it. "Why ever not? Isn't this much nicer than being a boring boy? Doesn't it make sense for us to be as feminine and pretty as we can? What kind of man do you think I'd make?" She put her hand back on the wheel.

"I guess. It's the same for us, I suppose."

"Absolutely! Don't you girls feel great right now, going out in public, being who you really are? Are you even nervous about it tonight?"

I glanced back at Franny. She was shaking her head. "I thought I would be, but it must be the drink. I feel nice tonight, and I'd never have guessed you were like us. I mean, you show such confidence in who you are and make people feel relaxed around you."

Jackie threw a quick glance back to Fran in the mirror. "And you will too. You'll see. By the end of the summer, neither of you will ever want to be your old selves in any way."

She pulled in front of the restaurant, and the valet opened my door, then Franny's, and went around to open Jackie's. Jackie took the ticket, placed it in her purse, and came around to us, clicking across the pavement in her heels. She was gorgeous in her black velvet, V-neck minidress. She held her arms out to her sides for us. "Ready, ladies?"

We each took an arm and walked in with her. The maître d' greeted Jackie by name and led us to a small table for three by the fireplace. We seated ourselves, and our legs grazed each other as we all crossed them beneath the intimate little table.

We perused the drink menu. Jackie ordered a Manhattan, and Franny and I ordered the fun-sounding martini called a Pink Princess.

Jackie observed the two of us. Franny was holding my hand on the table as she looked around the restaurant. "This is very nice. Thank you for bringing us. We can pay our share after."

"Not necessary. This is a business meeting, and it's in my budget. It's how I get to know my girls. Enjoy. Order whatever you want."

She watched as my eyes popped open, and my hand went up to cover my mouth. "Thank you!" Franny squeezed my hand and beamed.

Jackie laughed. "No problem. So, it seems you two are very close. Are you a couple?"

We looked at each other. We both shrugged and looked into each other's eyes. I placed my hand on Franny's as she held mine and said, "I think we are... kind of... I mean, we're roommates and really close friends, but we never talked about being a couple." I kissed Franny's lips lightly. "Are we, honey?"

Franny smiled, and her face flushed. "It's been what I wanted since the day we met. It seemed so gay, though, and I wasn't sure we'd ever be a couple, but being a girl right now, it seems... well, nicer. I'd love to marry you, Patty."

Our drinks arrived, and Jackie lifted hers to us. "Well, I guess I should toast the loving couple then." We clinked and sipped. "You know, though, you're very young to commit to such a thing.

Especially since you'll just be starting on the road to being women now. That could change things a bit."

Franny shook her head, leaned in toward Jackie, and grasped her hand as she looked into her eyes. "But see, we're not into men, and real girls wouldn't have us. So that's not an issue because all we have is each other."

Jackie raised an eyebrow. "Not into men? How odd." She leaned in close and whispered, "Don't you two ever have sex together? Make love?"

Franny blushed. "Uh, well. Not really. The most we've done is to give each other a hand... literally... now and then."

"Wow. Amazing. Okay. That's fine, I guess. Oh! I did get your lab results back, and you're both clean as a whistle, so you can feel safe if you want to have sex with each other, or other sisters—or any men guests at the sorority. All male guests are tested, too, by the way."

"Really? You test the visiting men?"

"Just the ones that we host parties with and so on. Like from a neighboring frat that we have a brother-sister relationship with. We gather with them from time to time."

Franny scoffed. "Ah! Now I get it. We're gonna be whores, and you'll make money off us."

Jackie grimaced. "Bite your tongue, girl! None of our girls will be whores. They'll be ladies, and no men will pay for them at our parties."

I slapped Franny's thigh. "See, Franny? You're always so negative."

Jackie smiled. "It's okay, Patty. I could see why she might think that, but I would recommend that the two of you take advantage of your clean and pure status with each other, at least. Girls like us need to know how to take care of men's parts properly and be able to make love to them. You owe it to yourselves to explore relationships like that and see if they're going to work for you. You do, after all, have the same plumbing as men. Besides, it will become second nature for you soon anyway. It's part of presenting as a woman. A lovely part. Just think about it a little."

I nodded. "Of course. We will. We can't wait—right, Franny?" I squeezed her hand on the table and ran my other hand up and down her silky thigh, caressing it. A grin came to her face. She pecked my cheek.

Jackie smiled. "I can see now that you two will love it."

4

We savored a delectable meal with a wonderfully matched bottle of wine, then had dessert and espressos. Jackie took us clubbing, and we all danced together until a few guys interrupted us, and we ended up dancing with them. Jackie bought us all a round of drinks, and we sat with the guys in a booth.

They were plenty polite, but it was strange having my stockinged thighs touching his and his hands slipping nonchalantly on my silky leg. I'm sure Franny and Jackie had the same treatment. The minidress made me feel so accessible to him. All he had to do was slip his hand under my dress, just inches away, and he'd know what I was. It was terribly frightening and arousing at the same time. Somehow feeling so susceptible was somehow feminine and nice—very sexy, like the vulnerable walk high heels force a girl to have. The guys were very complimentary, and Jackie ended the night after that shared chat and drink.

She held the car's back door open for us. "You girls did well with the men. It wasn't all bad, right? Let me chauffeur you two." We slid in the back and ended up cuddled to one side. I couldn't help caressing Franny's silky leg, and she did the same to mine. We were both quite aroused from the clothing, the drinks, and the excitement.

As she drove, Jackie said, "So ladies, thank you for going out with me tonight. I think we all learned a little more about each other, and I'm looking forward to living at the house with you both."

We thanked her fervently.

"It wasn't so bad having drinks with those men, was it?

I spoke up. "It was okay. They were quite lovely, really."

"Wasn't it nice getting the compliments and affectionate touches?"

I looked at Franny. She gazed blankly out the window while I squeezed and caressed her thigh, rubbing her hardness though her dress. I said, "I think I liked it more than Franny, but I don't think she hated it. Did you, Franny?"

She shrugged. "It was okay... I guess. A little scary, though."

Jackie smiled. "Good. At least you girls are on your way to becoming girls now. Good for you. I'm proud of you both. Now relax and feel free to enjoy each other back there, you two love birds. We'll be back home soon, and you can go to bed and have sweet dreams together."

I had a nice buzz, and I know Franny did too. I couldn't help but take advantage of riding in the back of that fancy car in the dark with Franny. She was so hot and sexy that night. I breathed in her perfume on her neck and whispered to her, "You're so darn sexy." I squeezed her gel breasts and kissed her neck lightly. She let out a little quiet whimper.

I slid her hand under my dress, and she slid it into my panties and wrapped her long-nailed fingers around my shaft. I did the same to her, and we kissed while we stroked each other. Our silky stockinged legs slid deliciously against one another. Our perfumes mingled. I whispered, "You're so nice and hard, Franny."

"You are too, baby. Your hand is so soft and warm too. Go slow. I want it to last."

"Me too."

I glanced at Jackie. Her eyes were on the road and not the mirror like I expected. Our bodies wrapped around each other in an embrace as we kissed and stroked tenderly and slowly. It was heaven.

5

Jackie pulled into the sorority driveway and parked in the back. Franny and I uncurled ourselves and got out, adjusting our dresses and running our fingers though our hair. Jackie stood waiting for us. "Thanks again for joining me tonight, ladies. It's nice seeing a happy couple like you two. See you both in the morning, ready to work, right?"

"Right," Franny and I said simultaneously. She took my arm, and Jackie motioned for us to go up the porch stairs ahead of her. Jackie went toward the bar. "Nightcap, girls?"

"No thanks. We need to get to bed." I laughed.

"Good. Go and have a wonderful night."

I held the rail as we ascended the stairs, and Franny held onto my arm. We entered our room and locked the door. I immediately grabbed Franny and led her to the bed. I sat her down and got onto my knees. I slid her panties to the side and gazed up at her. "I have to do this now. We don't have to worry, and I've always wanted to do this for you."

I took her hard little shaft into my mouth. Her hand rested on my head, and she looked into my eyes. "You look so pretty like that, Patty. Better than a porn star."

I nodded, smiled around her shaft, and mumbled a thank-you, looking into her eyes. I bobbed my head on her velvety rod and ran my tongue around it, tugging on her silky, smooth globes and watching her face respond. I could tell I was making her feel incredible, and it made me throb in my panties. Electricity ran through my titillated body.

She held my head tight and began to thrust into my face while looking in my eyes. She was as hard as a rock, and she let out a little moan. Then, all of a sudden, she took it from my mouth and lifted me up. She pulled back the covers to reveal pink satin sheets, and in the dim light, she slid onto the bed, pulling me with her. She lifted the hem of my dress, pulled aside my panties, and dove onto my rod, taking it in to her mouth. She attacked it as fervently as I had hers.

I watched in the dim light as it penetrated her adorable face, her eyes made up and wide, looking at me like a puppy. I thrusted into her face, squeezing her head tight. I couldn't take much more and pulled it out and moved away. "Oh god, Fran. Why haven't we done this before?"

I shoved her where I wanted her on the bed and slid over the silky sheets until we aligned our heads at each other's panties and consumed each other avidly. We moved in time with each other and dropped the pace to a slow, torturous one that might make the deliciousness last a while.

We did the same pattern to each other at the same time. Muffled whimpers came out of our full mouths, giving us an opera of sorts while we dined on pleasure, our bodies tingling and waves of ecstasy flowing though us and back into the other. It was as if we were one body experiencing all of it, wrapped around ourselves. Her excitement fed mine, and mine fed hers. Which was better? Feeling her excitement or being excited to give it to her? We fueled each other's energy.

Our perfumed bodies, the silky bedsheets and stockings, the high heels slipping and sliding... It was overwhelming. Somehow, we both knew when we'd reached the point of no return, and we both humped into each other's faces, then shot gushes into them. Our bodies clenched and spasmed. We both drank greedily as the shafts pulsed and shot in our mouths while our bodies twitched. Not a drop of that luscious, loving, passion-filled juice was lost between us. It was as if we replenished our stores of lust for each other by consuming every bit.

For a long time, we lay there, catching our breath, shrinking inside each other's warm, tongue-rolling, sucking, kissing mouths as we calmed and relaxed. When we were both soft, we slid around together, arriving back at our pillows. I kissed her forehead as she cuddled against me. "Nice having a queen-sized bed and not twin beds isn't it, Franny?"

"It's wonderful. I can't wait to wake up next to you. I love you so much."

"I do too. I love this. I love the new me." I caressed her hair, and we fell asleep.

6

I woke in the morning, and Fran was already in the shower. I lay there remembering the wonderful night we'd had together as two girls. Two girls giving up the guilt of a male-to-male relationship, letting go of old paradigms, and just enjoying each other like we should have always done. I felt a new, improved life stretching out ahead of us. I was hard and slid the pillow between my legs and began to hump against the satin pillowcase like an adolescent.

"Hey there, Patty. Stop that and get into the shower! We have a job to do."

I rolled onto my back and smiled at her. "Give me a little kiss first, *girl*."

She was tying her hair in a ponytail and putting it up on her head before the mirror. "No time. I'm starving too. Besides, what we did last night was plain disgusting. I don't know what ever came over us. The more I thought about it this morning, the worse I felt."

I sprang out of bed. "What? How can you say that?"

"It was bad enough that we gave each other a hand when we got desperate before, but last night was totally over the top, and we went too far. Guy roommates don't do that stuff." She slid into the jeans she'd worn the day we moved in and tucked her tee-shirt in. "Now go shower and get your painting clothes on so we can go down and eat."

I fought back the tears and got out of bed. My heart raced, and I was fuming inside. I stripped off my clothes and went into the shower, then did my hair, eyes, makeup, and lipstick. I came out and put on a pair of pink panties and a bra with the gel breast forms, a denim skort, and a bubblegum-pink V-neck tee-shirt. I put in earrings and added a necklace, rings, and bracelets, then sprayed perfume all over. I slipped into a pair of pink high-wedge-sneakers and tied them.

Franny was sitting in the chair in the corner, looking at her phone.

"Okay, Franny. I'm done. I don't think you'll get away with what *you're* wearing though. You heard Jackie last night. No pants. You don't even have any eyeliner or mascara on, and you look like a boy. I hope she doesn't kick us out."

"So what? This is totally wrong anyway. We're guys."

"I can't believe what I'm hearing! You'd throw this all away over your stupid, unfounded belief you're a man? You'd leave me!?"

Her face was frozen and turning red. Her lip began to quiver. Her eyes became watery. "I... I, uh..."

I stood in front of her and stroked her hair. "Relax. It'll be okay. Just relax and let's eat, and then you can change and we'll start painting. It'll be good for you. Being out in the fresh air and sunshine will relax you. Once you get dressed like you should, you'll fall back into it."

She shook her head and walked out. I followed her to the kitchen. Jackie was sitting at the table, her legs crossed, sipping a coffee and reading the back of a paint can. She wore an outfit similar to mine. She looked up. "Good morning, girls." She looked us both over, and a grimace came over her face as she observed Franny moving around and getting breakfast.

I sat down and poured a bowl of cereal and an orange juice. "Good morning, Jackie. I saw the look you made at Franny. Don't worry. She had a little breakdown, but she's going to change after breakfast and put on her makeup. Right, Franny?"

Franny sat and said nothing. She began to eat. She wouldn't make eye contact with either of us.

Jackie sipped her coffee and observed her. "Is that right, Franny? Are you okay now? Did you have some left-over portion of your imagined masculinity that got in your way?"

Franny's eyes flitted to Jackie and then back to her cereal.

"It's okay to have that happen, but a girl has to take control of who she is and do the right thing for herself. As long as you go back up and change into the girl you are, I'll forget I even saw this."

I patted Franny's hand on the table. "See? All good. You just need to take control like a big girl would."

Jackie wasn't buying it. She scoffed and stood. "Well, I can tell Fran is not cut out for this. If Fran doesn't comply with our rules, then she is not allowed to be on the premises. Will you comply or not, Fran?"

Franny stood, put her bowl and glass in the dishwasher. Her eyes were streaming tears as she ran out of the house crying. I stood to chase her, but Jackie held my arm. "Let her go. She'll either come to her senses soon or she's done. Don't waste your chance to have your dreams because she can't face her internal demons. Not all girls like us are capable of making the change for the better."

I sat down. I held back the tears and tried to calm my breathing to stop gasping. Jackie put her arm around my shoulder and held me to her. She patted my shoulder. "There, there. It'll all work out. You'll see. Just relax a little. Have a coffee. I'll get things set up so we can start painting." She kissed my forehead.

I looked into her inviting eyes. I saw her luscious painted lips and smelled her perfume. "Thank you, Jackie. I'm so sorry."

She ran her hand on my thigh, squeezing it and caressing it, sliding it up and under my skort. "It's not your fault, pretty girl. Just relax a little." She kept massaging my thigh almost to my panties. I throbbed. I looked at her luscious lips and leaned forward. I planted a kiss on her lips, and she placed her hand behind my head and kissed me deeply. She rubbed me thorough my panties while she kissed me passionately. She broke the kiss and looked into my eyes while she continued to grasp my hardness firmly. "There, there. Now isn't that better?

I nodded.

She squeezed and stroked my throbbing shaft through my panties and looked into my eyes. "Don't worry, princess. You'll be well taken care of here. You're gonna be one of the most popular girls in the house, I can tell. You're a natural." We kissed some more while she slid her hand into my panties. Her soft cool fingers wrapped around my hard shaft, and I felt loved and nurtured.

7

It wasn't long that I was able to relish the sweet feeling of Jackie nurturing and consoling me. Just as I was about to find release and relief from my grief and began to hump into her hand, she slid it out from under, slid my panties back over it, and stood up abruptly. "Okay. Let's go paint, girl. It's a beautiful day out there!"

She took the paint in one hand, my hand in the other, and led me to the front porch, my breasts jiggling from each step in my high-wedge-sneakers as a drip oozed from my begging shaft. "The ladder's in the barn when we need it. I have the tarps and brushes and rollers all here. Let's see how much we can get done."

We both started to get things ready, and then we moved the porch furniture and started painting. It was a gorgeous day, and whiffs of the fresh air, flowers, lilac bushes, and Jackie's and my perfume mitigated the paint fumes.

As I painted, my mind drifted away, from catastrophizing thoughts of my world falling apart with Franny leaving, to how pleasant it was to be doing what I was doing, dressed how I was, and feeling as feminine and pretty as I did.

I watched my hand, with its elegant, long, painted nails, as it held the brush and used it deftly and femininely, painting the creamy paint over the old, outdated, dirty mauve color. I was wiping out the old and bringing in a fresh new life for this house, remaking it into what it should be. Just as I was with myself.

I glanced over at Jackie, equally lost in the meditative state of doing her task. She was gorgeous, and I couldn't help but swell in my panties from looking at her tight bottom against her skort, her long legs in her modest wedge heels, her hair as it blew in the breeze, the smile on her fetching face. She made me feel even more optimistic.

I looked around the street, wondering if Franny was anywhere in sight, but she was nowhere to be seen. I'd miss her. A lot. I felt bad for her, but I was glad I hadn't done what she did. It would have been totally wrong. I was happy doing what I was doing and felt it deep inside of me.

We painted right up until lunch, then ate and went back at it. During that time, some other femboys arrived, and Jackie took them inside to talk with them and sell them on the arrangement. I saw excited faces running down the steps after each visit. At the end of the day, Jackie came out with two iced teas. "Done! That's enough for today, Patty. Take a break with me on the porch swing, and then we can get ready for dinner."

I took the iced tea, and we sat close together on the swing and set it lightly in motion. The air was the perfect temperature against my bare legs and rushed under my skort as we swung. "Did we get some new members today? They all had enthusiastic expressions as they ran off the porch."

"We sure did! Three new members. They'll all move in and go to dinner with us tonight. I think they're all going to be fantastic girls too. They're all so feminine already, and they were excited to be able to take it all the way."

She checked her phone. "Ah, blood tests are coming in already. It looks like they're all clean too. Perfect! Do you want a new roommate? I can put one in with you unless you want to give Franny a little time to clear her silly head."

"Let's wait a little. She might regret her choice soon. She might drive home and start her summer job, then realize what a mistake it all is and come back. If you'd let her, that is."

"Okay. Well, we can give her some time, but I'd hate to turn away even one girl who might want her space. We'll hold your bed for Franny until the last minute then. Unless of course you meet one of the girls tonight and decide you'd like to share your room with her. You let me know." Her hand glided on my leg, caressing it gently.

I placed my hand on hers and squeezed it. "Thank you." I guided her hand up and down my thigh and then let it go, and she continued to do it.

"Your skin is so silky. Not a bump or nub. I just love touching it." Her eyes radiated her sincerity. Was she falling in love with me?

"Thanks. It feels so nice, having you do that with your soft, silky hands."

"Mmm, yes, lovely." She slid her hand under my skort and into my panties, wrapping her fingers around my shaft and she stroked me. I leaned in and we kissed deeply for some time. She broke the kiss and continued to stroke while she gazed into my eyes and ran her other hand through my hair lovingly.

"Don't get me wrong, Patty. I like you a lot, but I know better than to get attached to any of you girls. That would be wrong for all of us."

"Uh, right. Of course."

"We need to keep your options open as long as possible. It's for your own good. For example, tonight. You should try to make love with one of the new girls. Did you make love with Franny last night?" She squeezed and stroked. I was so close.

"Uh, kind of. We sixty-nined each other. It was heaven."

"Oh good. So is that what flipped Fran's wig this morning?"

"Yeah. She thought it was all wrong. I can't imagine how she would have felt if we'd made love."

Jackie nodded. "Right. She'd be really freaked out. So have you used the attachment in your shower yet?"

"No. I was wondering what it was for."

"I'm sorry, I should have told you. It's for cleaning your bottom out after you poop in the morning so it's clean and ready for use."

"Really?"

"Absolutely. Girls like us only have only that one place to use like that, and it's best if it's clean."

"I guess that makes sense."

"Use the shower attachment tomorrow. Then you can plug if you want to get used to having something in there. You'll see how good it can feel. I'll leave one in your room for you later. I have lots of new ones for all the girls."

"Okay. Thanks."

"Good girl. You're gonna be great. But really—try to get close with one of the girls tonight. It'll do you good. Aim to try different ones all the time. I'm going to let the other girls know, too, that it's a good thing for them to practice that way and explore."

"Okay."

She slowed her stroking and kept me on the luscious edge with her soft warm hand. I thought about it as we swung in the fresh air. What a wild ride this might end up being! I'd never have imagined having so many partners that were all so pretty and feminine. Her hand and thinking about the possibilities had me oozing and lusting for them. I had to try the plug in the morning too. I just knew I was missing out on something. I could tell. I was just about to mess my panties and I looked longingly into her eyes and whimpered a tiny sound.

Jackie released her grip and slid her hand out then stood and gave me her hand. "I think that's enough caressing for you for now. Feel good?"

I took her hand and stood as I throbbed and oozed. "Lovely. Thank you. That was so kind of you."

"Oh you're *quite* welcome my dear. My pleasure. Us girls need to keep each other feeling nice. Nice job on the painting today, too. Let's go get ready, and I'll meet you at the bar for a drink if you like while the rest of the girls are getting ready."

"Sounds great. How should I dress?"

"We're going to the same place as last night. I have a driver for us tonight, and we can fit four in the back and one in the front, and we'll all be free to drink all we want. All set?"

"You bet."

I went to the room, took a nice bath, and shaved my body smooth. I dressed in a cream-colored, flared-hem, V-neck minidress.

I slipped on a pair of suntan pantyhose with the gusset cut out a bit for ease of access. Matching shoes and a lightly beaded, cream sweater with a ruffled cuff and puffy shoulders completed the outfit.

I curled my hair and draped it from a scrunchy at the top of my head and sprayed it to hold the shape. I did my makeup with my lips painted wet and luscious in a Cupid's bow with twenty-four-hour lipstick. I put in long dangling earrings, put on my rings, necklace, and bracelets along with anklet chains. My strappy patent leather stilettos had five-and-a-half-inch heels and matched the creamy shade of my outfit. I sprayed perfume under my dress, over my legs and hair, and checked myself in the mirror. I throbbed in my panties. I filled my purse, slung it on my shoulder ,and went down to the bar.

"Hey there, pretty lady!" Jackie called from her seat at the bar. She stood and went around back. "Dirty martini?"

"Sure." I sat in the seat next to hers and crossed my legs.

She poured my drink and placed it before me, then came around and sat back down. She swiveled in her seat until her stockinged leg touched mine, then toasted. "To a great night."

"A great night." I clinked and we sipped. Jackie's hand went to my thigh and began caressing it immediately while she looked into my eyes with her now made-up, night-look eyes that I imagined in the bedroom, or looking up at me while she sucked me. I throbbed a few times uncontrollably.

Her eyes roamed my face. "You're very... very... pretty, Patty."

"Thanks. I was just thinking how pretty you are too. Love your lips, your eyes."

"Penny for your thoughts. What else did you think about my lips? Hmm?" Her eyes flitted around my face as she smiled an alluring smile. She licked her lips.

"Oh god. Yes. You know exactly what I was thinking."

She laughed, then poked her tongue into her cheek, pushing it out. She laughed again. "You were thinking of me doing that to you, weren't you?"

I nodded.

Her hand slid under my dress and rubbed my panties as she looked into my eyes. She looked at her watch. "We have time."

She slid off the barstool and pulled me off mine. Then she knelt down, slid my dress back, and pulled aside my panties. She took me into her mouth and looked up at me while she bobbed her head, sucked, and ran her tongue in circles around my shaft. She tugged my globes, and I watched as I went in and out of her face. She was gorgeous. Seeing it go in and out of her ravishing face with her eyes on mine was incredible. I could tell she was enjoying it as much as I was.

It felt incredible, too, of course. I wobbled slightly in my heels, my knees began to get weak, and I held onto the side of the bar. I placed my other hand to rest on her head and began thrusting into her pretty face; her eyes locked on mine. She pulled off and it bobbed in the air and oozed a drip. She wiped the drip with her finger and licked it off. Glistening, it bobbed in the cool air a few times then stood there rigid and at attention waiting for more. I stared at it. I wanted to finish so badly.

Jackie stood and gave me a peck on the lips. "Put it away now, Patty. I want you on the edge for the other girls tonight."

I tucked myself away and heard applause.

All the new girls had arrived in the bar and had watched us. My heart raced, and my faced flushed.

"Welcome, ladies!" Jackie called out. "Seems you caught us enjoying each other a bit. Glad you liked it. We sure did. Feel free to do the same at any time in this house. Try not to finish anyone so you can savor the tension throughout the night. We're all one big family, and anything goes here. There's nothing to hide. It's all good. Keep each other feeling nice and... Very... *pretty.*"

She went behind the bar and began pouring drinks and making introductions. When she got to me, she said, "And this, girls, is the first member of this house, and her name's Patty. She's just gone through a hard time when her girlfriend broke up with her, so be nice to her tonight and make her feel nice when you can. She has space in her bed tonight, too, as long as her girlfriend doesn't come back, so see if you can't talk her into sleeping with you. It'll be good for her. Right, Patty?"

"Uh, yes." I forced a nervous smile, still calming down from being caught as we were.

We started chatting and drinking, and we all touched each other affectionately. Some of the girls sat and began caressing each other's legs and slipping their hands under each other's skirts. It didn't take me long to be hard again watching all the adorable girls being so sensual, their short dresses lifting and falling from the activity beneath them.

Before I knew it, I was working my way around, lifting dresses, taking the girls in my mouth, and looking up into their pretty eyes as I made them all feel nice. I brought one to the edge, then went to another. Jackie as well. It was like a dream come true. Others were doing the same, and I was brought to the edge by a very cute little thing with pigtails on the side of her head, which functioned really well as a means to hang onto her.

When it was time, Jackie called out, "Okay, ladies. Tuck yourselves away. It's time to leave."

In a flurry of clattering heels and giggles, we were off for the night.

Miss Pigtails got in front with the handsome driver, and immediately her head disappeared from view as a smile spread across the driver's face. He glanced down at her, then back out the windshield.

Jackie, the other two, and I were in the back seat, our legs slipping and sliding against one another and our hands all busy. It was a lovely ride to the restaurant, all of us making each other feel so *pretty*.

The valet beamed at us as he held the door for the parade of perfume, cleavage, heels, hidden raging hard-ons, and exposed stockinged thighs exiting the limo.

Jackie led the way, and the maître d' once again greeted her by name and led us to our booth. We all slid in cozily, and it was mutual leg-caressing time as we chose cocktails from the menu. As soon as we placed the orders, our hands couldn't wait to make each other feel pretty again. It was crazy, the level of arousal we were all feeling. I wasn't sure I'd last until after dinner.

"You're so pretty, Patty," Alexi said as she stroked me and I her.

"You too, Alexi. It seems femboys make better girls than girls do, don't they?"

"I know. This is a dream come true, isn't it? It seems too good to be true. Cheap rent and free clothes and being able to be as feminine as possible all day, every day. Oh my, Patty. You better stop, honey. I'm very close now and I don't want to lose it."

I stopped stroking and just squeezed it, looking into Alexi's eyes. "Are you sure? Why not let me wrap my dress around it and finish it? Maybe we can both get a little relief before dinner if you want to do it for me at the same time."

She looked around, then back. "Oh god, yes please, sweetie. I can't take it any longer. I won't be able to eat feeling, so... *pretty*." She laughed. She leaned in close, and I could smell her perfume as her eyes locked onto mine. She wrapped my silky dress lining around my shaft as I did to hers. We both stroked each other briskly, our legs slipping against one another. She whispered, "Huh, yes, that's it, little girl. You're making me feel so lovely."

Both our bodies shuddered as I felt her pulse and gush in my rapidly stroking grip, and I did the same in hers. She smiled broadly at me and took a deep breath, then gave me a peck on the lips. "Thank you. That was so nice." She squeezed my shaft once more; then we both let go of each other. She rested her hand on my thigh and leaned back in the booth. "Lovely." She observed the other girls chatting and touching each other while they sipped their drinks that had arrived while we were lost in each other.

I caressed her leg. "So, Alexi. Have you ever been made love to?"

"Oh god, yes. It's fantastic. Have you?"

"Not yet. Soon, though. I start plugging tomorrow."

"That's great. I'm plugged right now. Maybe later you can replace it for me with something else. If you'd want to, that is."

I hadn't even shrunk all the way before I started to throb at the thought of it. At that moment, Franny was the last person on my mind.

8

We finished dinner and had espressos and dessert. We didn't go clubbing because everyone was too anxious to get back to the mansion. Alexi and I were snuggled in the back seat, both of us looking forward to me making love to her. I was beside myself with anticipation of the intimacy, looking into her gorgeous eyes while I filled her and made her crazy. I thought about how much Franny would love it if she could just put aside her ridiculous paradigms like the other girls had—how delicious it would be for the two of us to be so intimately joined.

At the house, Alexi and I had a nightcap on the patio and then went to my room. We were much less wild and more affectionate, slow, and caring. We caressed and touched and kissed slowly and gently. The tension built and built and built some more until I couldn't take it anymore.

Silky legs wrapped around silky legs on the satin sheets; I maneuvered Alexi until she was on her back. I lifted the hem of her minidress and slipped off her panties, leaving the pretty, lacey crotchless pair beneath them, framing her rigid, shaved and silky package above her sheer black gartered stockings.

She pulled her legs back and held them open for me. My long painted nailed fingers guided my rigidness to her. She had already taken the plug out in anticipation and was lubed well. I pressed the tip against her, and she guided me in, pressing her bottom onto me. She was tight and moaned a little as she held my hips and paced my immersions. I held her legs back by her head and thrusted, making her high heels flail in the air. The look in her eyes, the way her silky shaft between us bobbed, leapt, and oozed, all showed me how good it had to feel to her. She whimpered a little and urged me to pick up speed.

I had plenty of stamina, and after having released a couple times already that evening, I was able to hold out for a nice long time. The sensation was incredible, feeling the connection to her and her body responding to mine. I wished it were Franny I was doing it with so we could have learned about it together, but Alexi was so lovely, receptive, and responsive… It was wonderful.

My phone rang on the nightstand, but I didn't look at it. I kept going. Alexi pulled my face to hers and gave me a deep kiss while I slowly slid all the way in, making her gasp a little through our kiss. I used short strokes to fill her all the way, realizing that taking it deeply made her gasp and whimper in pleasure.

The phone started ringing again with what seemed like an increased urgency. I didn't want to look at it. It made me angry, and I took it out on Alexi by pounding into her hard and fast. She called out my name and the word *yes,* over and over. The phone stopped ringing and after a moment began again.

Alexi turned and grabbed the phone, handing it to me. "Answer this fucking thing!"

I took it and leaned on one elbow answering it. "What!"

"Oh, Patty, I'm so sorry. I miss you so much. Please come home for the summer."

"NO! Come back here." I quickly went limp and fell out of Alexi. She tried to get me back in as I listened to Franny ramble on. It was futile.

Alexi rolled off the bed and grabbed her panties. "See you later, Patty. Maybe we'll have better luck another time. I'm going to see where the other girls are."

I rolled onto my back and turned my attention back to the phone. "Franny, just come back here before I'm given another roommate. New girls are joining every day."

"New girls? Was that a new girl who just said goodbye? Were you in bed with her?"

"I can't lie to you, Fran. As a matter of fact, I was making love to her, and I was just thinking how much I wished it was you I were with."

"Really? You were thinking of me?"

"Yes. I was. I wished it was you I was making love to. Now come home to me."

"You were making love to her!? Two boys dressed like girls? In his bottom?"

"Not his. Hers... her bottom. She's no more male than you or me. Yes. I wished it were you."

"Oh god! You're lost now."

"I'm not. You are. Come home and be the girl you're meant to be."

I could hear her choppy breath, her gasps, her breaking voice. "I don't know, Patty. It all seems so foreign and scary."

"Trust me, sweetie. You'll get past all that. Just come back. Before I get another roommate. I promise I'll help you. The other girls will help you. It'll do you good to be around other girls like us."

"Oh gosh." She snorted her runny nose. Whimpered.

"Please? It's you I love, Franny. Please? Be my girlfriend like we're meant to be. Love me so I can love you. You can get over your outdated beliefs. All the girls will help you."

"You think so? You think I can really do it?"

"I know you can. Now be a big girl and get in your car and come back to me. Don't make me come get you."

"Okay. Okay. I'll do it. Promise you'll be patient, okay?"

"I promise. It'll be so worth it."

"Okay Patty. I'm sorry. I'm sorry I'm so stuck. I'll really try to be a big girl, okay?"

"Yes. Wonderful. I can't wait."

"I'll see you tomorrow, sweetie."

"See you tomorrow, my love. I love you."

"I love you too."

I put the phone on the nightstand and plugged it in. I looked around the room and heard giggling down the hall. I was too wired to fall asleep. I went into the bathroom and cleaned myself a bit with a washcloth and tucked myself in. I fixed my hair, sprayed on some perfume, then went downstairs.

9

Jackie was sitting at the bar talking with another of the girls and having drinks. I sat next to her and poured myself a drink from the pitcher next to them, then seated myself next to Jackie.

"What's up, Patty? I thought you and Alexi had gone to bed."

"We had. Until Franny called and Alexi left. It was really bad timing. I feel bad for Alexi. I left her wanting more."

"Oh my, sorry to hear that. So what's up with Franny? She have a change of mind?"

"Yes, if you let her, she'll be my roommate again. I promised to help her with her paradigms and told her the other girls would too. Is it okay?"

"It'll be work for you and might be stressful."

"I know."

"She has to become one of the girls... completely."

"I know. She will. I'll make sure of it. She's sorry to feel the way she does and wants to become a girl like she knows she is."

"Good. Then I can't wait to have her back. Now relax so you can fall asleep. I'm tired and going to bed." She patted the leg of a darling, petite girl who was smiling, her legs crossed and one foot bouncing in her heels. "This is Cameron. Maybe she can help you relax a little."

Jackie stood and left, and Cameron slid onto the seat next to mine. She held her hand out daintily. "Hi! Nice to meet you, Patty." We shook hands. She leaned in toward me, and I could smell her perfume as her hand with its long painted nails glided on my stockinged thigh, and she looked into my eyes. "I'm getting tired. Like to sleep with me?"

10

The morning sunshine burst into the room. I looked around and saw the pillow next to mine was empty, and Cameron was gone. I checked the time—I should have been painting already. I hurriedly undressed and threw my things in the hamper. I pooped, showered, and cleaned out with the attachment. I plugged, did my makeup, and dressed in my painting skort and top and ran downstairs.

I went onto the porch, and Jackie was directing the new girls, telling them what to work on in the yard and garden. She had the painting stuff all set up. She came back onto the porch. "Good morning, pretty Patty! You look flustered."

"I overslept. Sorry."

"That's okay. It's understandable with what you had going on last night. Did you eat?"

"No."

"Did you use the attachment and the thing I left in your room?"

"Yes."

She looked me up and down smiling. "Good. How is it?"

"I haven't really paid much attention to it yet. It seems interesting, I guess. Not bad." I wiggled my bottom.

She laughed. "Good. When you're comfortable with the one you have now, I'll leave another for you that inflates and vibrates. It'll add to the interest and get you used to something more sizable."

"That'll be good. I want to be ready, and this one doesn't seem to do much."

"Did you turn it on?"

"I...uh, I didn't know it could be turned on."

"That explains why you don't feel it much. It's small anyway. It's just a starter plug. Good. You go eat and have some coffee. I'll leave the other one in your room, and you can change to that one, and then you can paint with me. Okay?"

"Thanks. I won't be long." She gave me a peck on the lips, and I ran off in my wedge sneakers.

After I was done with a quick breakfast, I couldn't help wondering about the bigger plug and ran up to my room. Jackie had left it for me, as she'd said she would. I quickly replaced the one I had and washed it off thoroughly, leaving it on the counter. It was cute to look at, all pink with a jeweled end on it.

I pumped up the one inside me while it vibrated in a pattern I had chosen, sending ripples of pleasure into me. I was hard and bobbing after it swelled up inside me, and I pulled my panties up, tucking my rod into them. I walked. Now... that was nice. It sent titillating vibrations and sensations through me with each step. If this was anything like what being made love to would be like, I was ready.

I walked onto the porch letting my hips sway with each step, and Jackie saw me. She smiled ear to ear. "Aha! You changed it already. I can tell. I see the glow on your face. Feeling pretty?"

"Oh my god, Jackie. I never knew this could feel so good. I feel very very pretty right now." I laughed. "I can't wait for the real thing. I'll feel *such* the girl *then and* so ...ha ha ha..*pretty*. I need to paint."

She laughed. "Yes. You'll feel so wonderfully feminine having the real thing leaving it's passion deep inside you. Think about that now. You'll see how fast time will fly today."

And it did. Before I knew it, it was time for lunch. All the girls ate together. Jackie had recruited two more members while I painted, and she encouraged everyone to make them feel welcome when they arrived. She also told the girls about Franny and her reservations and how to help her get over her old beliefs. I couldn't wait for Franny to return.

After lunch, I painted some more, and then Franny arrived. I put my brush down and ran down the steps to greet her. We gave each other a big hug and peppered each other's cheeks with kisses. It was so good to see her. "I have to go upstairs and change. I know the rules. I couldn't change at home or on the way, so let me do that first."

Jackie welcomed her back pleasantly and assured her she'd be fine. She sent us to get Franny settled in and changed and told her she'd be taking Jackie's spot and painting with me.

We got to the room, and I helped her find the denim skorts, top, and wedge sneakers for working. She went into the bathroom and did her makeup quickly, then came out. "What's that cute pink thing on the counter?"

"Uh, it's a trainer to help me get used to having something in my bottom so somebody can make love to me someday."

"Really? Why aren't you wearing it, then?"

"I'm wearing a bigger, inflatable vibrating one right now."

"Really? Eww! How's it feel?"

"Very nice, actually. And there isn't any mess because the attachment in the shower cleans it all up really well."

"Hmm." Her eyes took me all in, evaluating what I said. "Seems you're enjoying it. You seem to glow a bit."

I nodded quickly. "Yes. I can't wait for you to take the place of this plug when you make love to me. I can't imagine how good it will feel."

"I thought you slept with a girl last night."

"Well, I kinda did. But I was doing it to her and when you called, it was all over. She left."

"I see. So no one's made love to you yet?"

"Uh... no, not to me yet. I'm still learning with the plug. Besides, others besides you, well, that would just be some fun. Something to share and relax and have fun together with. It was very, very nice for me to be inside her, though, and I bet you'd love being inside me."

"Hmm. I like that you'd be *making love* with me. I like how that sounds... being inside you and how you'd see it as something really special when I used you like that." She came close and swept a stray hair off my forehead, then gave me a peck on the lips. "Let's get to work. I want to make a good impression on Jackie. I'll think about using you like that while we paint."

Now it seemed Franny was amenable to change and seemed to like the idea of making love to me. That would be even better even than Cameron was last night, even though that pretty, little, tight girl was totally taken with me, and I never had anyone so into anything as much as she was. To see her flailing little shaft spurting wildly as I spurted over and over into her beautiful tight little body was incredibly intense. I throbbed in my panties as the plug sent ripples into me, and I followed Franny's cute shaking bottom to the porch.

11

The day flew by, and soon we were getting ready for our first dinner in the mansion. Our chef and his crew had arrived and had stocked the pantry. Jackie instructed all the girls to wear identical dresses as a celebration of our first in-house dinner together.

Franny and I showered, shaved, and lotioned our bodies. I even convinced her to clean out and plug.

She whined, "Patty, I don't want anything in my bottom."

"But it's okay for you to put something in mine? Not that I mind one bit, and I'm looking forward to it immensely, but really—you're really into doing that to me, but you won't even wear a plug?"

"Of course I'll do it to you. Guys give anal to women. It's tighter for the guy, and women love it. You're darn close to a woman, and it wouldn't seem like I was gay or anything. Besides, I'm your guy, and you're my girl, and I can't wait to shove it into you."

"Franny! Listen to how you're talking. You're not a guy, and you make me sound like my purpose is just to please you as your girlfriend."

"Isn't it? And as far as my presentation as a girl, it's worth it to get the cheap rent."

"Don't let Jackie hear you talk like that, or you'll be out."

"Don't worry, honey. I learned my lesson."

"But you'll wear the plug so I'll let you stuff my bottom?"

"Sure. It's just a toy. It's not like it's real."

"Well, it's a first step at least. Okay. You can make love to me but only if you wear the vibrating plug. You'll see how good it is. You'll want the bigger one next."

"Whatever, girlfriend." She slapped my bottom.

So there it was… Franny was ready for shoving it into me, even though she wasn't ready for it for herself. That was the deal with the plug, though, and she willingly followed along and did what was necessary to get what she really wanted from me.

The dresses they had chosen for us were a bit over the top. They were petal-pink, lace-top V-necks with short crinoline skirts and white gartered stockings. Pink lace crotchless panties framed our hard packages, which were wrapped in sheer pink sheaths with the head poking out the top of the ruffled end. This allowed them to rub the soft pink crinoline of the dress. Our plugs moved seductively with each tiny step in our strappy pink stilettos with six-inch heels. Each tiny step heightened our arousal in our vulnerable, sensual ensemble. It was a well-planned outfit for girls like us, and it felt incredibly feminine, alluring and oh so *pretty*.

When we carefully made it down the stairs, Jackie had the camera set up for group pictures and individual shots. Even though we were all laughing and having fun in the group poses, it was a bit odd that she had us lift the hems of our dresses and show off our highly decorated and rigid packages while wearing big, happy smiles, showing how proud we all were. Every one of us was rock solid and bobbing up and down under those raised dresses—it was quite a picture indeed.

We sipped drinks and chatted, and we made our rounds from one to another, touching and feeling and helping one another to feel nice and pretty. I observed Franny through all of this, and she was the most reserved. She only felt another girl through her dress a couple of times, and her face turned red as she did. I leaned into her and said, "Don't be so shy, Franny. Get into it. Aren't they all, so enticing and sweet-smelling?"

"They sure are. Being a guy, I'd fuck them all."

"Franny! You can still do that. Why not at least show them a little graciousness and suck on a few? They'd like you more for that. Right now you're being very stand-offish."

Her eyes rolled back in her head. "I, uh... I don't know."

I took her hand. "C'mon. We'll do it together." I took her over to Cameron and started by myself as we knelt before her. Then I held it for Franny and moved her head toward it with my hand. I touched it to her lips. She looked up at Cameron, who gazed down lovingly. "It's okay, Franny. Go ahead. Please?"

Franny looked to the side and saw Jackie watching her. She reluctantly took it into her mouth, grimacing as she did, and Cameron responded with a girlish moan and whimper. She touched Franny's head gently, her body moving in her intensely sensual way. Franny let go of her hesitation and got into it. She loved how much Cameron was enjoying her ministrations. As time went on, Franny became almost frenzied until Cameron forcibly pulled her off and said in her tiny girl's voice, "Not yet. Not yet, Franny. Stop."

Franny stopped, a bit embarrassed and blushing. Jackie stepped in front of us, and Cameron moved aside. Jackie took Franny's head in her hands and pushed her rod into her lips. Franny began again, slowly and seemingly reluctantly. Jackie looked down into her eyes and glided her hand over Franny's head. "Good girl, Franny. You're such a good girl."

Franny nodded and mumbled around Jackie's shaft. She bobbed her head on Jackie, not looking at her. Jackie squeezed her head tight and thrusted into her face, giving her accolades all the time. Then she said, "Franny, you are a perfect receptacle. Real men will love you. Oh god, girl, are you ready for it?"

Franny's eyes went wide as she looked into Jackie's. Jackie whimpered and her knees shook. Her glistening shaft swelled as she thrusted into Franny's face and began depositing gush after gush, which Franny struggled to swallow. Franny's eyes widened, her body tensed, and she rose up on her knees as her hips thrusted under her dress. Even though it didn't appear Franny was into it, it had gotten her excited enough to release—whether she was fighting it or not.

When Jackie was done with her, she lifted Franny up from her knees and gave her a big hug and kiss on her forehead. "I'm very proud of you. You were reluctant at first, but you showed your inner passion, and you'll be very good with real men." Franny looked sheepish and embarrassed as she wiped drips from her chin. She looked away from Jackie and quietly said, "Thanks, Jackie."

Jackie walked off to mingle.

I stood up and adjusted my fluffy, sensual dress. "Franny, I could tell you actually finished, didn't you? Without even touching it."

Franny shrugged.

"That's wonderful! It shows you're believing you're a girl and love to give pleasure. It's natural that it makes you feel good. Relax. Dinner will be soon."

I took Franny by the hand; we went to the bar, and I poured us a couple of mojitos. Franny shot the first drink down and poured a second, then we relaxed as we watched all the girls enjoying each other in various ways. "Lovely, isn't it, Franny? I mean they're all so pretty and special."

She nodded.

"So Franny, are they girls?"

She sipped and swished the martini in her mouth like mouthwash, then grimaced and swallowed. She shrugged.

"Are you a girl?"

She looked at me sheepishly. "I am. I must be. I did that."

"Good. See? Another step is over with. Could you do that to a real man now?"

She shrugged.

"Of course you could and you'd feel so nice after. You're a big girl now." I gave her a peck on the cheek. "I'm so happy. I want you inside me. This plug is telling me how badly I want it. How does yours feel?"

"Good, nice. Subtle."

"We'll get you one like I have next. Then you'll be ready to receive."

"Hmm. Not so sure about that yet."

"How about making love to me?" I gazed at her lovingly, held her hand.

"I told you I want to stick it in you. You're my girlfriend."

"That's a good enough answer for now. Maybe you should do one of the other girls first."

"They're really still all guys."

"They certainly aren't, but if you don't want proof of physical birth gender you could always do it from behind and hide the proof in their panties. Look at those cute bottoms these girls have. Imagine those fluffy dresses lifted on their tight, peachy bottoms."

"Hmm..." She leaned into me, her hand caressing my leg. She uncrossed and recrossed her legs, slipping them deliciously against each other. She nodded and sipped her drink. "Yes. Nice tight girls' bottoms for sure. I'm in a cat house with a bunch of pretty pussies."

I hugged her arm and continued to caress her legs while we watched the group.

Jackie went to the center of the room. "Dinner is served, ladies. Please go into the dining room."

A table was laid out with food, plates, glasses, and gleaming utensils. We all took seats, and Jackie sat at the head of the table. The chef stood behind her. Jackie raised her wineglass. "Ladies, please toast our wonderful Chef Paul. He will see to your nutrition and the enhancement of your libidos with his special menu. Not that you need enhancement from what I've seen..." We all laughed. "But so you know, you will feel it more as time goes on. It will be a measurable difference. I want you all to start tracking the number of times you release in a day. No more holding back. I'll post a chart in the kitchen for you to fill out. We'll use today as a baseline. A toast to Chef Paul!"

We all raised our glasses and said, "To Chef Paul!"

He bowed and left, and we started passing the serving platters.

The girls all chattered about the libido-enhancing diet and giggled at the thought of it. The food was superb; the taste alone made one feel the sensuality food could impart. It all seemed so alive and rich in flavor and texture.

We dined fabulously, and when we were done, we all took a stroll around the garden in our fetishy high heels, walking in tiny steps, hand in hand, following Jackie, who was holding Cameron's hand.

After our walk in the garden, we went inside to the great room with the bar and fell into the couches. Everyone was a bit slower after the meal, and Jackie passed out espressos. Soon, the group was alive again and someone turned on music to dance to, while others played on the pinball machines, in a room to the side, or lounged on the sofas around the gas fireplace, or at the bar. It was a strange family of girls chatting, giggling, and having fun.

Franny was relaxed next to me, and I slid my hand onto her lap. She was hard again. "Feeling nice, Fran?"

She nodded and moved her hand to my lap, wrapped the soft crinoline around my hardness, and stroked me. "Mmm, very nice."

I slid myself into her lap and wrapped my arms around her neck. I gave her a wriggling lap dance. "How does that feel? Want to get inside?"

Her face flushed.

"I'll get rid of the plug and come right back."

"No. Let's go back to the room."

"It'll be better for you if Jackie sees. She'll know you've accomplished another piece."

"Right here?"

I looked around. "Look, see those girls against the wall? What do you think they're doing right now?"

She nodded and began stroking me faster. "Hmm, nice."

"Yes." I stroked her faster.

"Okay, go. But hurry."

I went to the powder room, removed the plug and washed it, touched up my hair, makeup, and lipstick, then perfumed myself. I went back down. Jackie was watching while Franny was sucking another girl on the couch next to her. "Good girl, Franny. Next time don't wait for me to tell you what to do with these lovely girls. You should be motivated to give pleasure that way. I shouldn't have to tell you to do it. All men will want it, and you need to be proactive. Anticipate their needs."

I sat down alongside them and watched. I stroked Franny's head. "Very nice, Franny."

The girl she was doing smiled at me and winked.

Franny sucked her dry, whimpers and little squeaks emanating from her. The girl arranged herself and gave Fran a kiss on the lips, then left to the bar. Franny seated herself and arranged her dress around her. I sat next to her. "Ready to put it in me?"

"She blushed. "I, uh… It's too late. I did it again when she gushed in my mouth. It was too exciting. Sorry, Patty. I failed you."

"It's okay. That's a good thing, discovering something you love to do so much that it gets you there just like that. It's wonderful." I kissed her forehead. "Later. There's lots of time."

We sat and I stroked myself while I watched everyone. Franny pushed my hand aside. "Let me do that for you, honey."

I sipped my mojito while Franny stroked me tenderly through the soft fluffy crinoline. I was getting very drowsy. I closed my eyes and just focused on the feelings and Franny caressing and stroking me slowly and tenderly. I was utterly relaxed and in bliss.

12

My mouth was full of firm, hard flesh, and my hips were being held tightly from behind. I heard voices as I absentmindedly sucked and worked on what I had in my mouth. It felt wonderfully firm and warm. I felt a stinging slap on my bottom, and then firm flesh pierced it. I gasped and looked over my shoulder to see Franny behind me as she thrusted hard and fast into me, her pretty face contorted. She wrapped my hair in one hand and held my hip with the other as she pulled my head back and pounded into me, grunting.

I felt something against my lips and opened my mouth to it and began sucking again. Franny pounded me repeatedly, grunting and shoving as if she had a score to settle with me. She wrapped my hair in her fingers so tightly it hurt. Other hands held my head tight as the shaft pierced my lips and mouth over and over in a frenzy.

I was on all fours on the carpet in the great room. Girls were all around me, stroking themselves and watching us. They egged Franny on to go faster. She did. I was flailing under my dress, the soft crinoline like electricity against my shaft. I was on the edge so much it felt like one continuous release as I oozed and oozed. I moaned around the shaft in my mouth and uttered little whimpers as they both penetrated me, one at each end.

It was like a dream of some sort, utterly surreal. That dreamlike state felt endless, but then I felt Franny as she shoved it deep into me and held it there. The one in my face did the same, and they both dumped their loads into me, one gush after another. I felt splashes landing on my face and my bottom from others. I couldn't help but tense up and shake and release all my pent-up passion from my shaft, which was flailing beneath me.

I collapsed on the floor, the one in my mouth shooting a stream on my hair as it fell loose. Fran collapsed on top of me. I caught my breath. I opened my eyes and looked to the side to see

Jackie's high heel and her hand. "Come, Patty. Let's get you two to bed. You were both incredible. Was it good?"

I nodded.

Jackie touched Franny's shoulder. "Franny, are you ready to be the recipient? Do you want what Patty just felt?"

"Yeah, right," she snorted.

We helped each other up the stairs and fell asleep quickly on our own sides of the bed.

13

Every morning, I'd shower first and clean out. Then, after I was made up and dressed, Franny would take me while she was after her shower, wearing a wife beater tank top with her hair pulled back tightly. She'd slip behind me, take the plug out, pummel me, while grunting and slap my bottom. When she was done with me, she she'd say what a good lay I was, or how tight my pussy was, or what a great little sissy bitch I made, and then finished getting dressed.

Morning after morning, she did that. I wasn't the only one either. The charts Jackie had told us to fill out in the kitchen showed Franny at the top of the list. Her graph shot upward, and all her releases were in the bottoms, from behind, of the girls we lived with. She was a monster at twelve times a day, while the rest of us hovered around seven. She popped them off in the backyard, on the patio, in the house… I was amazed the other girls all obliged her when she approached them, but she was *soo* good, they couldn't resist her, and they could count on her to give them a release too. She was rather long and thick compared to the rest of us, for sure. But she was also brutal and derogatory like an angry man might be.

We weren't talking much and the other girls didn't chat with her either. She had gone off into her own world. The house was now full, at the twenty-girl capacity, and we had other special dinners where pictures were taken. Jackie wasn't saying anything, but I could tell she wasn't pleased with how Franny was acting. Even though she dressed the part well, she was more like a rooster in a chicken coop than a girl.

Then, one day hairstylists came in to color, perm, highlight, or cut—whatever the stylists determined would give each of us the most enduring feminine appearance. When Franny's hair was done, there was no way she could look in the mirror and ever think she was a guy. Her long hair was permed and colored in a palette of blonde, red, and chestnut streaks with an intermingling of bright sissy pink. She couldn't ponytail it, pull it back, or do anything that would convey masculinity in any way. It framed her angelic face, and even without any makeup or lipstick, she was obviously all girl.

I loved my new hairstyle. It was also supremely feminine and was full and rich in colors and waves. I felt like a princess, and it changed my demeanor and boosted my feeling of femininity by ten times. My makeup, nails, and presentation all became sexier.

We were getting ready to go down to dinner one night. I had put on a cute pink flowered mini-sundress with matching heels and gartered stockings. I fluffed my hair and sprayed perfume all over me as I checked myself in the mirror.

Franny came out of the walk-in closet in a tight black V-neck minidress with black high-heeled boots and her hair gelled down. She came up behind me as I adjusted my earrings.

"Hi, Patty. You look very feminine and sexy tonight. Like the rest of the girls. I really love this place." She breathed on my neck and bit my earlobe. Her hand lifted the back of my dress. My plug was barely out before she was in and placing the plug on the dresser. She grasped my hips tight and pushed me to the floor on all fours, where she rammed me over and over while tugging my hair and slapping my bottom. "That's a good girl, Patty. Take care of your man. Aren't you glad you have me to keep you in shape?"

She wasted no time and didn't allow me to even have a moment of pleasure from her penetration before she froze and clenched, pulling my hair and releasing her pulsing passion into me. As soon as she was done, she pulled out and quickly shoved the plug back in.

I caught my breath, stood up, and composed myself while she tucked herself away and went about loading her purse with lube and makeup. I wiped tears from my eyes. "That was nice of you but, Franny, I was wondering when you might take some time and make love to me? I mean, you do that, and it's nice while it lasts, and I'm so happy to make you feel good, but it just feels like I'm your flesh-light. It would be nice to have some time so you could go slow and make love instead."

She glanced at me then turned away as she spoke. "That was the third with you today and my eleventh. I'm going for a record tonight. I can pop off at least two more, and I'll be the leader of the house in that test."

"Franny, it's not a test. I don't know how the other girls let you do that to them either. If it's like mine was, they aren't getting a release from it anymore either."

She laughed. "They don't care anymore. They know what their purpose is now, and they just get on their hands and knees and get it over with. They're food for the alphas like me."

"Jackie's gonna catch on, you know, and then she'll toss you out. You're a wolf in sheep's clothing."

"I'll cross that bridge if I ever get to it. She's just watching the release charts, and I'm winning right now."

We went downstairs, had a sumptuous dinner as usual, and afterward, while Franny moved around going for her record, Cameron and I took turns making love to each other back in her room. Slowly, gently, back and forth, taking turns. One of us was on her back gazing up into the eyes of her lover, then the other. It was heavenly. I hit a high of eight for the day and little, sensual Cameron hit eleven. Both records for us.

At the end of the evening, everyone gathered back in the bar. Jackie handed out little pink-wrapped presents to each of us, then stood in the middle of the room. "Okay, girls. After the last month, your graphs seem to have plateaued these last few days. I'm very proud of you. Your bodies have become used to such busy, rewarding days, and now it's time to reap other rewards. Your gifts are e-stim chastity cages with automatic regulation. They'lll bring you to the edge and may even be able to keep you there most of the time without any release. You must put them on as soon as you soften the next time. Bring the keys down and deposit them in a box that will be in the kitchen. You won't need to post anything on the graphs anymore because for a while, there will be no release. You'll no longer need to plug, but you must practice the same daily hygiene and always be ready." She looked around the room.

Cameron raised her hand. "So we can't plug? Or we shouldn't plug?"

"Can't. We don't want to risk that setting you off accidentally. No more releases for the near future."

Cameron whimpered and held her hand to her mouth. She looked like she'd cry. Jackie stepped over to her, placed her hand on her shoulder, kissed her forehead. "Yes, I know. It will be hard. You'll feel more feminine and *prettier* than you ever did. You" be so very hard in the tiny cage with only one way for you to have relief. I have relief coming, though. This will make sure it's the best experience you've ever have. You'll never feel prettier then when it happens to you then."

14

Franny was furious. She stripped naked, got into bed, and rolled onto her side facing away from me. I placed my hand on her shoulder. "It's okay, sweetie. You'll see. It'll help you be the girl you are. I was never able to be inside you and make love to you. I doubt any other girl was either, right?"

She nodded and covered her head with the sheet. I pulled it back and kissed her neck. "It'll be fine. You'll love it once you've done it. You've worn the biggest vibrating plug day after day already. It won't hurt a bit."

"That's a vibrating plug, a toy—not the real thing! I'm gonna be stuffed and used and dumped in like a flesh-light."

"You do that to me, and it's not at all bad. It would be nice if you took your time, though, and thought about my feelings."

"I know it's not *all* bad for you. That's because I'm a guy, and you're a girl, and you're supposed to be sub to me. Now what am I gonna do? Just take it from him?"

I took a deep breath. "Look in the mirror and see what you are. Give up your stupid notions of manliness! Be that girl in the mirror... enjoy life."

She tossed and turned. Flipped and flopped. Then she came close to me and nuzzled against my back. I hadn't even taken my clothes off yet, and I tried to get out of bed. Franny pulled me tight to her and nibbled my ear. She was hard against my bottom and stroking between my cheeks. I wriggled my bottom against it. "That's it, honey, make love to me. Please? Nice and slow. Tell me you love me. Make me feel feminine and pretty."

She slid into my already lubed and used bottom, and I felt her enter. "Mmm, Franny, let me face you so I can see your alluring eyes." I tried to roll over. She held me tight and stroked into me slowly.

"That's nice too. Just like that. I can feel your passion, your love." I began to ooze with each stroke, and I rubbed against the silky lining of the dress with each thrust she made into me. "That's it, Franny. Keep going slow, and we can come together."

All of a sudden, she grasped my hips tight, lifted my bottom off the bed and pounded herself into me over and over, and then she clenched. I felt her pulse inside me. As soon as she was done, she slapped my bottom and rolled onto her side, facing away from me again.

She turned her head. "Thanks. I needed that, bitch." She took a deep breath and drifted off to sleep. I lay there, hard, unsatisfied, bobbing in the air, wishing for her to change. I told myself the cage would do it for her. I imagined her making love to me like she almost just did, and I let my thoughts linger in the part where she was caring, loving, and making love to me. I spurted into my dress and fell asleep.

15

In the morning it was the usual routine of Franny exerting her dominance over me by using me as a depository. After she was done, I grabbed her wrist. "Now put on your cage when it softens."

"What!?"

"You have to, Fran. It's the rules. They have pictures of us, you know, the bylaws. You're stuck. Don't start another argument. Just do it, like the man you think you are! Suck it up like a man if you think you are one. Please?"

I adjusted my mini-skirt and top after my pummeling. I looked at her. "I'm gonna take care of my hot-and-bothered self because you, as usual, didn't take care of me, and then I can put on my cage. You should put yours on right now."

I sat on the bed and closed my eyes. I grabbed a pair of panties, imagined Cameron making love to me and shot it off in the panties. I put the tiny pink electric cage on, squishing myself into it as it softened. After it was on all the way, the lock clasped, it seemed to have a mind of its own, and it turned itself on and ran through different patterns, making me jerk and twitch until it settled into one that felt wonderful. Too wonderful. It didn't allow me to get soft at all, and I quickly filled the tiny pink cage tightly.

I pulled my panties up and looked at Fran. She had put her cage on and was staring at it. "Not bad. Nice toy. All guys should own one of these to stay ready for action."

I shook my head. Franny got dressed and did her makeup, and then we went downstairs.

We were down to painting the detail trim now, and the house looked fabulous. The yard and gardens were brought to their maximum beauty, as had the twenty girls working, laughing, and having fun being girls at work. Of course, we all knew how pretty we felt with our new presents from Jackie, and we knew there was nothing we could do about it now that our keys were all in her possession, so we grinned, very widely, and bore it.

We wore the cages for a week, shaving around them gently, replacing the batteries, keeping them fresh and clean and pretty. Someone had the idea to decorate them with bows and ribbons, and we all did except Franny. No one could look at them and think they were anything but cute, insignificant, tiny, and feminine.

Franny was beside herself with libido. All of us were, but she just wanted to use anyone for her receptacle and get it done. With the cage, that was quite impossible. She still hadn't grasped the fact that the only way to find relief would be to *be* the receptacle. She was in a vile mood, sliding her stockinged legs against one another, caressing them when she could, fixing her hair over and over, squeezing her breasts. You could see the libido just rippling in her body, but she wasn't getting any closer to wanting what she needed to.

That weekend, there was a special surprise dinner. Once again, we had to wear a special outfit. This time it was a bridal outfit. It was similar to the little pink ones with the six-inch-heels and crinoline, but in all white with white bejeweled headpieces with the veils draped back. These dresses, however, had the ruffled front hem styled up high enough so one didn't have to lift it for the group pictures. Our tiny cages were on display again, all decorated except Franny's. I felt pretty as a princess and was proud to be wearing my decorated little cage, which kept me right on the edge.

We all were chatty and touchy-feely with each other, but it only made us more and more aroused in our tiny cages. We'd had enjoyed a couple of cocktails when Jackie came to the center of the room and asked for our attention. "Ladies. As you can tell, it's a very special night, with you wearing your very special bridal outfits. This is your graduation to full womanhood, and we have special guests to help you all celebrate. Please welcome your admirers who have been following your progress through my emails since the day of your arrival."

In walked about thirty handsome, young men, all dressed in black tuxedos. The girls gasped; many covered their gaping mouths while others, wide eyed, just let their jaws drop.

I looked to Franny. She was standing next to me in shock. Her face was red. A tall, stunning black man came into the room; he looked around, and as soon as he saw Franny, he approached us. He put his hand out to each of us in turn. "Franny and Patty. I've been following you two, and you're such an interesting couple of roommates." Franny glanced away from his beaming smile and his eyes as if he had an unwelcome power over her.

He still held my hand as he gazed at Franny. "She's stunned," I explained to him. "We weren't expecting men here tonight. Very handsome men, at that."

"Thank you, Patty. My name's Wolf Blaze. You two are the most interesting girls I've seen in the group. I'd like to get to know you both better if that's okay."

Jackie approached us. "Yes, like I told you, Wolf—they are very interesting. They make such an unusual couple. Please, meet them, talk with them, explore them thoroughly, and then let me know what you think." She turned to Franny and me. "Yes, you might have guessed, girls. We've been advertising the sorority to a number of men who have an interest in women like you. Wolf has a keen interest in Franny... and you too, Patty. You're somewhat a contrast to each other, and he thinks you'd pair well together. Now do your best to make Wolf happy, ladies."

I throbbed in my electric cage imagining what it might be like having a real man like Wolf make love to me. He was elegant and graceful—clean-smelling, smooth-shaven, perfect creamy coffee skin, and handsome as hell. I could see the sizable outline in his pants, and I could all too well imagine it unveiled. I throbbed and oozed in my cage.

Franny looked like she'd seen a ghost. Her skin was pale, even with the makeup, and she looked like she might retch. I put my arm around her and whispered, "It's okay, you're ready. Put your mind on the longings you feel...your need...your desperate need. ..How totally pretty you feel. Forget everything else. Think about satisfying that craving. He can help."

Wolf brought us drinks like a gentleman and gave us his arms to hold as he led us in our fetishy high heels, us taking three steps to every one of his. Our gel breast forms jiggled, the cages tugged, our hips swayed, and the breeze swept across our legs and cages as they did their e-stim routine. We sat with him on a couch on the patio, crossing our legs and bouncing one foot. He caught me staring at his crotch. "Something of interest, my lady?" He rubbed it and smiled. "Maybe I'll let you both meet it intimately later. Let's chat a little while we enjoy our drinks and this beautiful weather, and let me savor your lovely company."

I couldn't help but smile at him and place my hand on his thigh. "Yes, that sounds wonderful, Mr. Blaze, sir—"

"Please, Patty. Wolf."

"Okay, Mr. Blaze—I mean Wolf—so tell us about *you*. Tell us how this all came about and why you're here. I take it we've been advertised, and men like you are interested in girls like us. So many men too." I looked around at all of them chatting with the other girls.

"Yes, well, it's quite a story if you're interested. Let's see, where do I start? I suppose I should start with myself. I'm a psychiatrist by degree. I was always interested in investing, though, and as soon as I had extra money, I invested in digital currency. You know, Bitcoin, Ethereum, Dogecoin. It was so low priced in those days and had so much potential, which minimized the risk at the time. With the dramatic price spikes, I began taking profits. Elon Musk was about to go on *Saturday Night Live,* and everyone thought he was going to plug Dogecoin. I knew he wouldn't because he's such a brilliant yet unpredictably crazy guy, so I dumped it and took my *80,000 percent* gain!"

He laughed. "I could have stayed in a little bit longer, but as I'm sure you both know, it's better to get out when you can reap the benefit and forgo a little of the upside than to lose it all. What do they say? A bird in the hand is worth two in the bush. Like your girls' investment in yourselves while here. You could have passed on this opportunity, but the risk was minimal and the potential was good. A wise and frugal investment of your energies." He paused and sipped his drink, looking at us both.

Franny was bouncing one of her stockinged legs over the other and caressing it with her hand while she sipped.

I touched his leg again. "So you're worth a fortune now, huh?"

"Yes. I no longer practice psychiatry because I can make so much more just investing what I have, even conservatively. That allows me to make more of an impact on those who need it rather than simple counseling. For example, I made the investment in this sorority to help all the femboys out there who might need a little help becoming what they might *really* want to be. After counseling several, I became interested in their plight and felt I could be of assistance in their journey of discovery. Jackie has been wonderful in her diligent pursuit of this goal, and I couldn't have done it without her. She was one of my patients at one point. She made me the most aware of what was needed and what could benefit you girls."

Franny glared at him. "So you're the devil who is doing this to us men!"

Wolf laughed. "Devil? Try saint. Franny, I know you're reluctant, but it's merely old paradigms clattering around in your head. You are what you are and will never be what you aren't, so why not accept it and enjoy it? Look around at the girls here. They're all delighted to be in this family. Unfortunately, in any family there's always one child who seems to fight everything. You are her."

"I'll never accept it."

"Jackie told me that she recommended ejecting you early on. I told her to give you time... for Patty's sake. I know how much Patty loves you. I think you truly love her too, but you're fighting it right now."

Franny looked sheepish. I held her hand in both of mine and rubbed the back of it. "Admit it, Franny. Please? What's the truth?"

She just smirked and sipped her drink.

I reached for an oyster on the iced platter on the side table and slurped it off the shell. "Mmm, nice. So... you're rich and made this sorority, which is heavenly for someone like me. Who are all these other men? Did they come to use us girls or what?"

Franny scoffed. "You made a cathouse... You've made whores of us."

Wolf shook his head and smiled warmly at Franny. "No, my dear. Here's the offer all these men will make to the girls they're interested in: They're all rich and have tremendous resources and are looking for women like yourselves. They'll sign a contract with a specific girl or girls for the remainder of her college career. The contract says nothing more than during the time taken for the extent of your schooling, however long you choose to go for, even if you wanted two or more doctorate degrees...it says that your room and board, clothing, tuition, and transportation will all be paid for, and you'll also receive an allowance. Bodily changes such as implants and cosmetic surgery are covered as well if you want them."

My jaw dropped and my hand went to cover it. "That's fantastic."

Franny looked shocked. "What's the hitch?"

"You must live with the person you signed the contract with during that time. That's all. If at any time you want to break the contract and leave, you may. No strings attached. You just lose your benefits. It is simply an opportunity for girls like you to blossom and men like us to be with girls like you, who might fall in love with us and grace us with your beauty and charm for the rest of our lives. Does that sound like a cathouse?"

"Hmph. I guess not." Franny looked at her long, painted nails, holding her hand out and moving it about to admire it.

"See, Franny, how you're looking at your pretty hand? Do you think that's a sign of masculinity?"

She stopped and bounced her leg, caressed it with her hand gliding up and down it. She took a deep breath, straightened her back, glancing down at her cleavage. "I, uh... but..."

Wolf laughed. "Sorry, I'm not laughing at you. I can just see the struggle you're having internally, and I also see the girl is much more prevalent in you than the man."

I laughed. "You think so, doctor? Really? Isn't she too masculine and manly for a girl?"

"Don't make fun of her, Patty. She's struggling."

Franny scoffed. "I'm a femboy, not a girl."

"Okay. So what does that really mean?"

Franny broke down and started to sob. I put my arm around her shoulder. "It's okay, honey. It's okay."

"I know what I am. I know I'm a girl. I just don't want to lose myself. It's as if I'm giving up control."

"Is it really? Or will you only be in control when you take control, as the powerful, strong-headed girl you are, and kick out your evil, demanding, interfering, social construct of right and wrong?"

She took a deep breath, and it seemed she melted into Wolf's eyes at that moment. She put her arm around me and pulled me close to her. She gazed lovingly into Wolf's strangely-light-blue eyes. "I know I've been wrong. When you talk about control, that's the key. I've been thinking I have to be in control, and to do that, I reject the things that are right for me. Things I feel that yell at me me who I am. I fight who I am because of a social construct of men and women... I hate my fucking dad and all the men and the society out there that made me this way!"

Wolf took a deep breath. "Okay, Franny. Congratulations. You've broken through the wall now, and you're on your way to freedom. You understand your reality and know how to fix it." He looked at his watch. "I think it's about time for dinner, so we should all go get a seat. That is, if you girls would be interested in talking about your futures with me. You could talk to any of the men here and pick others, but they had all picked out the girls they wanted to spend time with already. I guess the question is, am I a nice enough guy to get to know better?"

16

Dinner tables were set up everywhere to accommodate us all —in the dining room and on the patio and porches. We were on the patio in the fresh air, seated at a table for the three of us. I held my quail-egg sushi appetizer before my lips. "So Wolf, education. Anything and it's paid for?"

"Yes, there are good schools around all the interested men's homes. You could transfer."

"Do we have to stay in the same major?"

"Of course not. Be who you want to be. That's what we're offering. A chance to become anyone you want. Why do you ask? Would you switch? Franny, what's your major?"

"We're both going for engineering because those are the best paying and most needed occupations."

"Engineering? Congratulations, girls. Those are tough majors. Of course you can stay in them or change."

I dabbed my lips with my napkin. "I'm changing mine right away. This year, if I can get into the next school quickly enough. It is the end of the summer."

"A little donation can go a long way toward admission, but why change?"

"Who wants to work that hard? Now that I have you to help be my backstop, I can do something more fun. Clothing design, art, digital design. Who knows?"

"Good choice. You should take the opportunity to be who you want to be. That's what this is all about. Franny, you could change too."

"Maybe. Engineering is really manly and respected, though."

"Women are in engineering too. You'd still be respected."

"I suppose. Clothing design does sound fun."

"See?"

I sipped the wine. "Where do you live?"

"In a mansion of sorts in Massachusetts. Plenty of good schools there. Don't worry—I have gardeners and housekeepers, and you girls wouldn't have to lift a finger. Just be who you are and be my friends... and lovers if you please."

I melted at the thought. I was oozing in my cage. I could imagine being with Wolf forever. "Do you work anymore, Wolf?"

"Not a lot. Just for my own entertainment. The money keeps growing on its own, really. What I'd like to do is travel the world, spending lots of time in one place at a time to really get to know the culture, foods, sights, weather, all of it. Then I can choose where to retire when I'm ready. Of course, I wouldn't do that until you girls are done with the schooling you want."

Franny's eyes lit up. "Travel the world? That was one of my goals. That's why I wanted a job to make good money, so I could take a trip every year."

Wolf laughed. "Well, young miss, when you've reached your goals for schooling, we can do that if you want to stay with me." He turned to me and grasped my hand on the table. "You too, of course, Patty. Both of you. I'd like to keep you two lovely ladies together unless you two grow apart."

Franny turned to me, her face animated and excited. "Patty, let's just quit school and travel. That'll be more of an education than anything. Wolf will take care of us, and we can be together forever."

I was shocked to hear her excitement and willingness to be the girl she is with Wolf and me.

"Franny, slow down. Are you really ready to be with a real man—and me, of course—for life? I mean, Wolf has to be treated well, and we'd be his lovers. Could you do that? Don't be so quick to throw away an engineering degree and be the girl if you're gonna regret it."

"Wolf showed me my problem. I understand it now. It all makes sense. I want to be a woman... almost. I mean I want to get implants in my butt and breasts and hips and cheeks and all of it. I want to be the girl I always wanted to be. I could never get rid of my little friend, though." She looked down at her cage then back at us. "It is still a necessary part of my mind and body. If that's okay with you, Wolf." She looked at him pleadingly.

He laughed. "Of course it is. It's part of the deal."

"Well, my mind is made up. I'm ready. You and Patty and I will travel the world."

"Okay. Then let's enjoy dinner and we can become more intimate after and see how you feel. Okay, Franny... Patty?"

We both nodded quickly and excitedly and grabbed each other, giggling.

17

Dinner and chatting with Wolf was fabulous. He was a fascinating guy and thrilling to be with. He was a few years older than us but not too old at all. Just mature and stable. Very stable in every way. He seemed genuinely interested in our futures and in us as persons. Franny seemed to look to him as if he were a father figure, judging by the way she listened and took in his comments. She seemed to be falling in love with him.

After dinner we sat on a couch on the patio, drinking espressos. Wolf was between us. I leaned my head on his strong shoulder and slid my hand over his crotch, feeling him and rubbing him while we all gazed at the sunset and relaxed. I reached over and took Franny's hand from caressing her own leg and moved it to Wolf's crotch. She smiled at him, and her eyes lit up when she felt him hard, thick, and long beneath the pants. She grinned up at him. "Oh my god, Wolf. You *are* a beast—and not only in name."

"Yes, I've been given many gifts, and that happens to be one of them. Don't worry, I'll be gentle... until you want it different."

"Franny, go ahead and show Wolf how good you are with your mouth."

Jackie was walking around checking on everyone, and she stopped and watched as Franny took Wolf's zipper down and took his whole shaved, creamy coffee package out in the setting sunlight. She wrapped both hands around it and still hadn't covered it all. She took what she could into her mouth and began bobbing her head and stroking with both hands. I reached over and tugged and rolled his hairless, silky balls around. Jackie smiled and moved on.

Wolf held Franny's head lightly and leaned back. I kissed him deeply, my legs sliding against one another, my breasts tugging on my chest. I smelled Wolf's manly cologne, and my e-stim cage made me ooze as I throbbed in it. I wanted him so badly.

I broke the kiss and looked at Franny. She was fervently working on Wolf, and I could tell how much she was enjoying it.

Wolf tensed up and squeezed Franny's head tightly. He grunted. "Oh, Franny! Ready?"

She nodded quickly and mumbled around his thick, dark, and glistening meat thrusting into her face, gazing up into his eyes and stroking him with both hands.

Wolf shoved his hips upward and held it there, looking into her eyes, his hands cradling her head of hair. I could see the gush as it made its way through the long pulsating shaft... through her hands and into her mouth. Her eyes went wide, and she swallowed hard. Some leaked onto her fist; another and another went through it like a firehose, and she diligently swallowed one after the other, her eyes locked on his and her legs sliding against one another.

When it was done, Wolf slumped back and let out a deep sigh. Franny let go and diligently and carefully cleaned her fingers off and licked his shaft clean. Then she dried it carefully with a linen napkin as if she worshipped it. He worked at tucking it all away while she watched it leave like a lover going away on a plane. She continued to stare at it after he had it tucked it in.

Wolf laughed and lifted Franny to kiss her kips deeply. "That was lovely, Franny. Thank you. I'll have you know, I don't expect you to do that all the time."

She laughed. "That sucks. I want to... and more. I want you *in me* next time. I want to feel it. I have to. This cage is driving me mad. I never wanted anyone inside me, but now I know I'm all girl, and I feel *sooo* darn pretty right now, and I want you, Mr. Blaze!"

Wolf laughed. "You're crazy, girl! I love it. But I must think of Patty too. Right, Patty?"

"Darn right, Wolf!" I ran my hand over his pants and felt it. "Get that beast back here now."

I rubbed it slowly and kissed him deeply. Franny crossed and recrossed her legs over and over, felt her breasts, caressed her legs, and was going crazy with desire. I knew now she truly did want it.

She had changed. Wolf had changed her. I might lose her. But I wanted Wolf too.

I took him back out of his pants and began on him with my hands and mouth. Soon, I got him from flaccid to hard and ready. I took him by the hand and started to walk inside. Franny followed.

I led him to our bedroom and made him stand before me while we stripped every stitch of clothing off his David-like body and placed him on the bed. I slid in beside him and lay on my back, my head on the pillow, and I lifted my legs back. I pulled aside my panties and reached out for him.

He moved closer and pressed the tip against me. He pressed while I tugged and pushed my hips onto it. I never thought it would fit, but after a few minutes and a little stretching, it made its way past the gate and I gasped.

"Is it okay?" he asked.

I nodded while it stretched me to the limit. "It should fit. I used an inflatable for a long time, and it fit. Just push slowly." He pushed and pushed, and it inched its way in. He held my ankles back by my head. Franny peppered my face with kisses and squeezed my breasts as she watched it go in.

"Make love to me, Wolf. Show Franny how it's done."

He stroked it lovingly, gliding in and out in slow strokes. Each thrust made me ooze from my cage a bit. I squeezed his hard ass and made him go faster. I was on the edge, electricity racing through my whole body, from toe to head from the passion he was filling me with.

He lifted himself above me, and Franny held my legs back. My high heels flailed in the air above me as his speed increased, his eyes locked on mine. My cage flailed and drips fell off it into the air.

"Be the beast, Wolf!" I cried out. "Finish in me."

Wolf pounded it long and deep into my body. It felt as if it would come out my throat as his breathing accelerated and his thrusts got harder and faster. All at once I began to feel waves of pleasure all through my body; the e stim cage somehow seemed to know I was ready, and I began to have a full body orgasm, jerking and shuddering and spurting long ropes from my cage into the air between us.

I felt Wolf tense and pulse inside me, filling me with gush after gush, his eyes riveted to mine. It was as if we were one. I felt every bit of his passion, and I was sure he did mine. I whimpered with delight as my body shook. When it finally subsided, and I stopped twitching and jerking, Wolf fell to the side of me. Franny stretched out on my other side and draped her legs over mine. She kissed me repeatedly on my cheeks and head. "You were so beautiful. I want to make you feel that good."

I turned my head and kissed her forehead. "Do you want Wolf to make you feel that good too?"

"I do. But I owe you. I owe you so much now for getting me to stay. I owe you my life. You put up with so much bullshit from me. I love you. Be my girlfriend forever, and I'll be yours?

"Of course."

Wolf ran his big hand over our backs, massaging us both as we lay there wrapped around each other. "Relax, ladies. Relax and love life. We have a long and happy one ahead of us."

If you enjoyed this book, it would be great if you could leave a review and tell a friend about it or blog it out. Thanks!
Barb and Thom
For more of books, both fiction and non-fiction, go to:
Amazon:
http://www.amazon.com/Barbara-Deloto/e/B00J21HWA4/